T0117486

Take Paws to Laugh!
A Purrade of Funny Cats
from Flabby Tabbies
to Sour Pusses!

Hilarious
Cat Riddles
Cat Jokes
&
Catoons
Created by
Mike Thaler
America's Riddle King

Books by Mike Thaler

CATZILLA: *Cat Riddles, Cat Jokes and Catoons*
MONSTER KNOCK KNOCKS
OINKERS AWAY! *Pig Riddles, Cartoons and Jokes*

Available from MINSTREL Books

CAT RIDDLES, CAT JOKES AND CATOONS

(Original title: *Paws*)

Created by
MIKE THALER
America's Riddle King

PUBLISHED BY POCKET BOOKS

New York   London   Toronto   Sydney   Tokyo   Singapore

**For Susan and Ben
Purrtners**

Originally published as *Paws*

This book is a work of fiction. Names, characters, places and incidents are either the product of the author's imagination or are used fictitiously. Any resemblance to actual events or locales or persons, living or dead, is entirely coincidental.

A Minstrel Book published by
POCKET BOOKS, a division of Simon & Schuster
1230 Avenue of the Americas, New York, NY 10020

Copyright © 1982 by Mike Thaler
Cover artwork copyright © 1990 by Tom Hachtman

All rights reserved, including the right to reproduce this book or portions thereof in any form whatsoever. For information address Pocket Books, 1230 Avenue of the Americas, New York, NY, 10020

ISBN: 978-1-4814-2543-8

First Minstrel Books printing January 1991

10 9 8 7 6 5 4 3 2 1

A MINSTREL BOOK and colophon are registered trademarks of Simon & Schuster

Printed in the U.S.A.

STARRING

THE ~~CAT~~

MOUSE

Ar-cat-tecture

The Leaning Meower of Pisa

The Purrthenon

Westminster Tabby

The U.S. Catpitol

Edinburgh Catsle

The Golden Gat Bridge

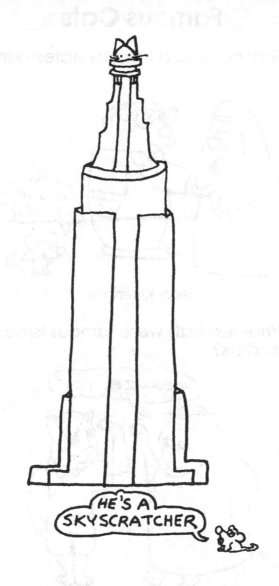

and the Empurr State Building

Famous Cats

What cat was a famous statesman?

Henry Kittenger

What two cats were famous Israeli leaders?

Golda Meower and Meowshe Dayan

What little cat was a famous bandit?

Billy the Kitten

What cat was a famous Iranian leader?

The Meowatollah Catmeany

What is a famous expression of "Valley Cats"?

"Pawsome!"

What cat is a famous super hero?

Catman

What cat was a famous astronomer?

Cat-purr-nicus

What famous cat discovered America?

Christo-purr Cat-lumbus

What cat is a famous Cuban revolutionary?

Fidel Catstro

Name a famous newscatster.

Dan Ratter

Cat Crosses

1. What do you get if you cross a cat with a night bird?

2. With a small talking bird?

3. With a pickle?

4. With a melon?

5. With a donkey?

6. With a mouse?

7. With a cow?

8. With a Band-Aid?

9. With a small mean fish?

ANSWERS

1. A meowl
2. A purrakeet
3. A sour puss
4. A cataloupe
5. A mew-l
6. A meowse
7. Cattle
8. A first aid kit
9. A purranha

Cats in the Arts

Name two great cat sculptors.

My-cat-angelo

Claws Oldenburg

Name four great cat painters.

Meowtisse

Clawed Monet

What Kinds of Cats Are These?

1.

2.

Catdinsky

Jackson Polecat

3.

4.

5.

6.

ANSWERS

1. Hip cats
2. Hub cats
3. A push cat
4. Corn on the cat
5. A cat-o'-nine-tails
6. A rock-cat

The whole kitten caboodle

How Puss in Boots Outsmarted the Ogre Almost

Cat Favorites

What's a cat's favorite room?

The kit-chen

What's a cat's favorite color?

Purrple

What's a cat's favorite indoor sport?

Rat-cat ball

What is a cat's favorite game?

Tic-cat-toe

What's little cat's favorite rock group?

New Kits on the Block

What's a cat's favorite magazine?

Rodent Track

What's a cat's favorite sports car?

A Meowcedes-Benz

What is a cat's favorite holiday?

Cat'smas

What's a cat's favorite department store?

Meowcy's

What are a cat's two favorite Italian dishes?

Meownikitty

and veal catlets purrmesan

What's a cat's favorite movie?

Catsablanca

What's a cat's favorite place in the whole world?

Lapland

Cat Presidents

Can you name these four U.S. cat presidents?

3.

4.

ANSWERS

1. Tom-meows Jefferson
2. Tabby Roosevelt
3. Jimmy Catter
4. Dwight D. Eisenmeower

Cat Definitions

Cat-tankerous

...ry-corner

Catter-act

Cat-a-tonic

Cat Monsters

Frank-cat-stein

The Hunchcat of Notre-Dame

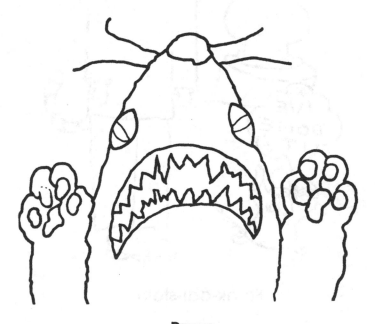

Paws

The Meowmy's curse

Cat Dracula

The Kitten from the Black Lagoon

The Invisible Cat

Cat Kong

Catzilla

and the Wolfcat

Cat Imitations
or
Mask-cat-raids

Can you guess what this cat is imitating?

1.

2.

3.

4.

5.

ANSWERS

1. A pig
2. A mouse
3. A turtle
4. A fire hydrant
5. An umbrella

Cat Superstars

Who is a cat's movie heartthrob?

Tomcat Cruise

What cat starred in *The Godfather*?

Meowlin Brando

What cat played a great movie gangster?

Jimmy Catney

What cat played a grand lady?

Catrin Hepburn

What cat became a legend?

Meowerlyn Monroe

What cat is one of the world's great directors?

Federico Feline-i

Cat Riddles

What kind of cats make the best sandwiches?

Cold cats

What do cats put on a hot dog?

Cat-chup and meow-stard

What do you call a cat that ties itself in knots?

A cat-tortionist

What do you call a cat that won't eat a shark?

Fin-icky

What do you call a cat with an alligator on its shirt?

A purr-eppy

What do you call an electric cat?

A circat

What do you call a Spanish cat that fights mice?

A cat-ador

What do you call a Spanish mouse that fights cats?

A mata-dormouse

What do Spanish lady cats play?

Cat-stanets

Where do cats keep their money?

In a kitty kitty

What kind of cat is white and soft and sweet?

A marsh-meow-low

Where do little cats get their ice cream?

Catskin-Robbins

What do weight lifter cats have a lot of?

Meowscles

What do you call a cat that starts a party?

A catalyst

What do you call thirteen screaming cats?

A catter-wall

What are cat sweaters made out of?

Catsmere

What cat is constantly picking up mice?

The crosstown puss

What kind of cat is afraid of heights?

A scaredy cat

Cat Rulers

Strange Cats

Can you identify these cats?

1.

2.

3.

4.

5.

ANSWERS

1. A caterpillar
2. A kittypillar
3. A catbird
4. A catfish
5. An octopus

New Joke

Old Joke

What happened to the three French cats whose boat sprung a leak?

Un deux trois quatre cinq!

Cat Geography

What mountain range is this?

The Cat-skills

What river is this?

The Meowsissippi

What three cities are these?

Cat-tongue
Sen-sen-catty
and
Paw-kit-see

What city has the happiest cats?

Mew Orleans

What three South American countries have the happiest cats?

Purru, Purr-away and Purrzil

What two states have the most cats?

Connecticat and Cattyfornia

What are a cat's two favorite oceans?

The Catlantic and the Pussific

What island is this?

Cat-aleana

Cat Knock Knocks

Knock knock.
Who's there?
Alley cat.
Alley cat who?

Alley cat for Christmas was a yo-yo.

Knock knock.
Who's there?
A Persian.
A Persian who?

A **Persian** to see you.

Knock knock.
Who's there?
Tabby.
Tabby who?

Tabby, or not **tabby**
That is the question . . .

Knock knock.
Who's there?
Siamese.
Siamese who?

Siamese jokes are pretty bad!

Knock knock.
Who's there?
Abyssinian.
Abyssinian who?

Abyssinian you in a little while.

More Cat Riddles

Where do cats send their problems?

To Dear Tabby

What do you call it when a cat listens to a mouse's problems?

Psycatanalysis

What do you call it when cats march down a street?

A purrade

What do you call a cat in a pot?

A catserole

What do you call a cat's cold?

A puss-nasal drip

What do you call it when a cat names her four new kittens Jack, Jane, Joan and Jim?

A-litteration

What does a cat say when it's hurt?

Meow-ch!

What does a cat say when it sneezes?

What does a cat wear on his chest?

A Cattoo

What do little cats wear when they go to sleep?

Pawjamas

What cat cuts the grass?

A lawn meower

What cat bends the easiest?

A Silly Putty cat

What cat has the best manners?

Eddie cat

What cat has the worst manners?

A slob cat

How do cats order in restaurants?

A la cat

Cat Rhymers

What do you call:

1. A disheveled cat?

2. An overweight cat?

3. A cat conversation?

4. A comic cat?

5. An urban cat?

6. A young cat in love?

ANSWERS

1. A shabby tabby
2. A flabby tabby
3. A kit cat chitchat
4. A witty kitty
5. A city kitty
6. A smitten kitten

A Cat in History

Catilla the Hun

Cats in Sports

Who is the famous cat sports announcer?

Howard Catsell

Who is the great cat tennis player?

John Meowkenroe

What are the two great cat professional football teams?

The Dallas Meowboys
and the Meowmi Dolphins

What is the great cat sport?

Mice hockey

What is a cat's favorite position on a baseball team?

Catcher

What do you call it when you throw a cat?

A forward puss

What game do tall cats play best?

Bas-cat-ball

Cat and Mouse

What car does the world's coolest cat drive?

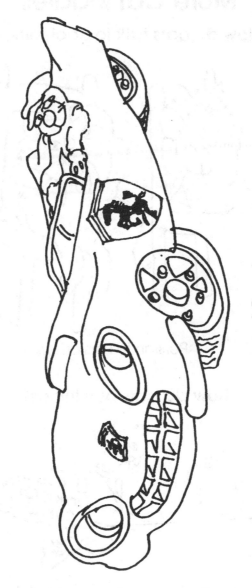

A Purrari

More Cat Riddles

How do cats talk to each other?

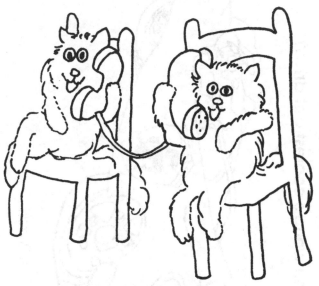

Persian to Persian

How do cats buy things?

With Cat Blanche or A-merry-cat Express

What's the occupation of most cats?

Mewsician

What is every cat?

A meows-trap

What cats give out tickets?

State true-purrs

What do you call a cat that carries golf clubs?

A catty

What were the two great cat empires?

Meowsopotamia and Purrsia

Who were the first cats to come to America?

The Purritans

What is the favorite car of rich cats?

Cat-illac

What do you call a very poor cat?

A pawpurr

What do you call very rich cats?

Aristo-cats

What kind of butterflies do kittypillars turn into?

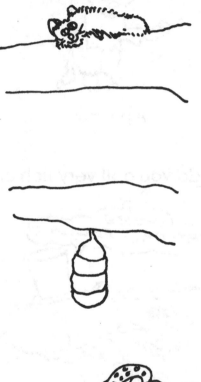

Meow-narchs

Where do cats go on vacation?

Meowmi

What cat holds up the world?

Catlas

What Kinds of Cats Are These?

1.

2.

3.

4.

ANSWERS

1. A cat-a-log
2. A cool cat
3. A bottle cat
4. A well-bred cat

Cats in Litterature

What is the great Russian cat novel?

War and Puss

What is the great American cat novel?

Meowby Dick

What is the great French cat novel?

The Cat of Mousey Cristo

What cat was a great lover?

Catsanova

What cat was a great pirate?

Long John Silver Tabby in
Kitnapped

What cats were great heros?

The Three Meows-cat-teers

What Do You Get?

What do you get if you put a cat in a Xerox machine?

Dupli-cats

What do you get if you put a cat in a blender?

A happy mouse

What do you get if you put waxed paper over a cat and hum?

A catzoo

More Cat Crosses

1. What do you get if you cross a cat with an ice cube?

2. A cat with a clam?

3. A cat with a vacuum cleaner?

ANSWERS

1. A cool cat
2. A purrl
3. I don't know, but it sure drinks a lotta milk!

Two More Knock Knocks

Knock knock.
Who's there?
Meow.
Meow who?

Tell **meow** to get in.

Knock knock.
Who's there?
Mouse.
Mouse who?

I **mouse** see you.

More Riddles

What do lady cats use to smell good?

Purrfume

Where does a lady cat carry things?

In her purrs

How do cats wrestle mice?

Catch as cats can

What do you call the cats' martial arts?

Karatty and cat fu

What does a cat whistle when he looks for a mouse?

A catchy tune

**What swims in a river,
has a lotta teeth and goes meow?**

Alley catters

**What else swims in a river,
has a lotta teeth and goes meow?**

Crocatdiles

**What swims in a river,
only has two teeth and goes meow?**

A hippopotapuss

**Who is the famous cat on TV that
changes words?**

Litterman

Cats in Meowsic

Name two great cat composers.

Meowzart

and Tchaicatsky

What cat was a great cellist?

Pablo Catsals

What cat was a great tenor?

Catruso

What voice parts do lady cats sing in opera?

Catralto and meow-so soprano

What two cats were great rock 'n' roll stars?

Elvis Purrsley

and Cats Domino

Name three great jazz cats.

Louis "Scratchmo" Armstrong
Felineous Monk
and Ella Catsgerald

What cat was a famous Beatle?

Paul McCatney

Famous Cat Sayings

When puss comes to shove

THE END

SELF-PAWTRAIT

THE AUTHOR

MIKE THALER, America's Riddle King, is the creator of Letterman, the popular Electric Company character. He has written and illustrated over eighty books for children, ranging from original riddle and joke books to fables and picture books. *Redbook* has called him "one of the most creative people in children's books today." His Minstrel titles are *Catzilla: Cat Riddles, Cat Jokes and Catoons* (original title: *Paws*); *Oinkers Away: Pig Riddles, Cartoons, and Jokes;* and *Monster Knock Knocks*, which was written with William Cole.

Mike is also a sculptor, a songwriter, a game designer, and an educator who has created a bookmaking and a riddle-making process for groups of children and their teachers. He is a sought-after speaker and has given many workshops and programs for children and adults across the country.

Above all, he believes in creativity—in himself and in others. As Mike explains it: "That is my life and my work."